THE LAST LOCAL

A WORLD IN ITSELF

MEGHNA MUKHERJEE

Copyright © Meghna Mukherjee
All Rights Reserved.

Thoughts are the seeds that helps a writer write her story. Imagination is resting somewhere deep. Sometimes a knock is needed to wake them up so that the image takes a form of a book.

A big thank you to my Mother, Mrs. Anjali Mukherjee who was tired of me continuously relaying story plots but stopped mid-way for the stories that did not match my expectation. Yet, she encouraged me to pen them down for she believed that the ideas would generate once I start writing. Thank you, Ma.

My son, Nimesh Mukherjee would cry for my company but his mother was lost in her world formulating a story but not writing one.

Lastly, my readers, my friends, and well-wishers. They were eagerly waiting for my next vivid or crazy imaginary stories and few motivated me to move from my genre of a murder mystery. Thankful to them for they wanted to read my next story.

Thank you to one and all, who have been constant supporters through my journey. After a long time, I enjoyed writing and I hope that you, my readers love the storyline. A means to keep the imaginary challenge going and increase my reader database or my fan following.

Thank you,

Meghna Mukherjee

Contents

I

Scene 1

Gazing at the fading lines at the horizon, Kirti felt as if a part of her was saying goodbye. Tears streamed down her eyes everything seemed blurred. The honking of the cars, the gushing waves, the singing of the returning birds to their homes, and pedestrians rushing from one signal to the other running to catch their modes of transport that would transport them back to their loved ones while Kirti stood staring blankly at everyone, moving around in a jiffy.

Kirti stood at the brink of the beach. The silent waves touched and caressed her feet. It used to be a moment of joy making her forget her day's worry but today it pricked her and made her emotional. She stretched her arms as if calling for the grey skies to engulf her and wash away her pain. Standing there for minutes, she felt no change. Her emotions over powered her rational thinking making her feeling dumbstruck and worthless. She knew it was not the end of the world but yes, a setback. A setback that she knew she would hardly be able to recover being surrounded by the best family she could ever ask for. If only her boss would understand her plight, but what else she could expect from the work front? After toiling hard for months but being unsuccessful and with a warning, today she was given the pink slip. Thanks to her emotional turmoil her productivity had gone on a toss and today she stood, jobless and it looked like she was alone in the whole wide world. She did have a family, but..., friends but... who could she share the pain with.

As the street lights made its way lighting the dark streets, Kirti knew it was time. It was time to head back home to face the reality. She had to be ready. Ready to face whatever the consequences the pink slip would bring to her life. Flipping a tear drop away, Kirti smiled murmuring, "Its time, now"

II

Scene 2

She walked through the familiar sidewalks and stopped at the regular hawkers, her favorite being the kurmura fellow. "Bhaiya, ekdum spicy baniyega" (Make it very spicy). The young lad looked at her confused. Firstly, Kirti never enjoyed spicy food. She always reminded him to make it less than medium spicy but tangy. Secondly, she would always speak to the young boy inquiring about his studies and family, and guide him too. Though he was asking her about the Math problem, Kirti was lost looking at the dark sky as if trying to find a ray of silver lining. Without being aware she just walked away with her packet, without paying for it and without saying a thank you.

While she was hurrying towards the platform, she could hear the phone ringing. As she was getting late, she ignored the ringer, but the caller did not ignore her. Kept on buzzing and that irritated her and slowed down her pace. She did have a phone but it was just a namesake piece that found some space in her handbag but not in her life, as no one bothered calling her nor did she bother calling anyone. Yet today someone was so concerned that the phone just did not stop buzzing. As she was getting late and it was time for the last local to leave, she was running instead of walking and she climbed and alighted the fleet of steps two at a time and once because of the ringer disturbance, she was hanging in mid-air but thanks to the railing she caught her self on time before she tripped and broke a bone or two but she did twists her ankle but she had no time for moaning as she could not miss the local.

Just as she breathed a sigh of relief, she found herself facing an empty platform, rather, an empty track. "Where is the local?" she questioned herself looking around every inch as if it was a toy train that had slid in between gaps. "I am sure, I had heard the announcement clearly saying, 5 minutes for the local to leave." But there was no train. What was the announcement, that stated the train leaving? She looked around, but to her dismay, there was no one except a dog who was stretching himself ready to hit the bed anytime, and here she was waiting for the last local, or had she missed the local? Waiting for a few minutes, she decided to exit and take another transport home when the loud sound of the whistle jostled her. The motorman was grinning at her as if happy to have found her. What was shocking was that the train was filled with few passengers who did not alight the train. To Kirti, it seemed as if they were on the journey for a long time and had a long way to go. The worse was that she was the only one waiting at the platform to board the train. All in all, it seemed that the train had returned to pick her up as if the motorman knew that she had missed the train. Nodding her head, she was about to step on the passage-way, when her phone buzzed. This time her hand vibrated forcing her to answer the call. Just as she was about to say, "Hello", the honking of the train indicated that the local was about to leave, so either she boards the train or she answers the call. She had no time to decide as the caller was screaming over the speaker, "Hello... Hello.. Kirti, you there. Hello... Answer. Kirti..."

Just as she said "Hello", the last local zoomed off...

III
Scene 3

"Kirti, Kirti… How are you? Where are you? Hope all ok. Why are you not speaking? Kirti… Kirti… Say something baby please.. Kirti?"

"Something is just not right." Thought Kirti to herself. Just to be sure, she checked her caller id to check whether it was the same person she was listening to.

"Kirti… why are you not speaking. Talk dear. I am tensed now." The speaker went on. Kirti was unable to hear. Maybe a network issue, but can a network issue change the tone and feelings. Probably, a cross-connection.

"Are you Kartik?" she asked twitching a brow. She knew the answer. He would have disconnected the call, but No, he was still there inquiring about her and her whereabouts.

"Kartik, I am fine. It is just that I wanted to spend time at the beach. My favourite place you know after… (She hesitated before speaking about her pink slip) I am travelling back. (Looking at the wristwatch) I know it is late but sorry.."

"Hey dear. Don't be. It is just fine. After all you…"

The speeding sound and the gushing winds were making it impossible to hear what Kartik was saying. Whatever she heard, she felt it next to impossible to believe. "Was it Kartik, really?" she kept repeating the question while flipping her phone.

Trying to forget what had happened, she closed her eyes to relax, but Kartik's sweet and concerned words kept ringing in her ears and she was unable to forget it. She knew something was wrong, but unable to understand, she plugged in her earphones and played her favourite music. Yet, her mind was playing the voice of Kartik. She was restless, unable to focus on the music nor was she able to relax closing her eyes. Scanning the pictures, she knew what she wanted. At once, she unlocked her phone and hit the speed dial saying *"Hi.. Dear.. I"*

IV
Scene 4

"Hi… Dear. How are you? I was missing you and thought of speaking rather wanted to share this with you. I got a pink…"

Before she could finish her statement, the line was disconnected. She kept staring at the blank rather disconnected screen wondering why? *"Maybe network issue"* saying which she dialed his number, but after a ring, he disconnected the line. She wondered what the issue was and feeling dejected she kept dialing again and again to face the same fate, the line was being disconnected. After a few failed attempts she found his phone switched off.

"Now, what do I do? He never behaved in this way with me before. Whenever I wanted him, he was there." He always said I was more than a friend, a family. Then why did he just *switch off on me."* She was unable to stop the tears from flowing. Not even once, in their decade-long relationship did he avoid her. Whatever time, season or occasion and place it was, he was there in a fraction of a second, and unless and until she felt good, he never left her alone. Her smile was everything to him and he would go to any limits to get that smile back on her face, even if it meant breaking

open an ice cream shop in the middle of the night, and here he not just disconnected the call but switched off his mobile. *"Why was he avoiding her?"*

Kirti did not have to wait long for an answer. Her restlessness was put to rest within minutes. Just as she was contemplating calling him again, he messaged her.

"Meet me in 10 minutes. Same place. Don't be late"

She was happy that he had responded, but just a line, a message. *"Why did he not call and worst, why did he not pick her up? How will I travel alone at this hour? What is wrong with you? Wait, till I meet you and give you a piece of my mind."* She spoke aloud to herself while she walked to the venue happy that at least he was meeting her.

While she was waiting, she scanned through her gallery. Photographs that, always brought about a smile on her face and they were a reminder that life had another side as well. A side that she enjoyed but it was hidden. Kirti believed that certain aspects of life must well be hidden. If revealed it could be taken in a wrong manner. She did not wish to lose her other side of life, her happy and cherished moments.

V
Scene 5

It all started a decade ago. Precisely, just 6 months after her so-called happily married life. Kirti thought she was the luckiest when she tied the lifelong knot with her childhood buddy and a successful IT professional Kartik Arora. Hardly did she know that what looked colorful and bright on the outside had hues of grey from the invisible side.

It was one of the most important day of her life. All that she had worked for, her success and career depended on the success of the presentation and approval from the heads. She had prepared well in advance taking no help from anyone. As such in terms of context she did not need help. She was weak in terms of technology and had asked her hubby for help, who had kept promising for a long time but till the last minute, was just unavailable. Kirti was now in a fix. The next day she had to present her work, but the statistics were missing and Kartik had raised his hands. After a huge round of arguments with Kartik, she picked up her laptop and headed straight to the nearby café. Sipping coffee filled her with a ray of hope that sparked a change in her and she was able to deal with the issues at hand. Yet, this time the caffeine had no effect on her spirit. She tried to ask for help from Google, but the technical words did not help her and she felt everything was just slipping away from her hand.

"Madam, here is your 25th cup and it's a request please don't sip into any more caffeine, or else you will throw up. By the way, I am Amit Tandon, a software developer and from the far end, what I noticed was that you were struggling with some statistical tools and slides. If you don't mind, can I help you? Though I am a stranger, I am safer than another dose of caffeine."

Ignoring his features, Kirti at that time was thinking of just a solution, and without a second thought, she agreed and within 30 minutes her work was done. In her excitement, she forgot to thank him. The entire night she prepared for her presentation while hubby dear was snoring throughout.

The next day, the presentation was a success. She was given the promotion that was long awaited yet she was unable to crack the deal. "Work hard but focus on market research," said her team lead. She knew what was expected of her. She tried to call her husband to share her success story but as usual, he was unavailable. She wanted to call the stranger but just like the word, he was a stranger indeed as Kirti neither had his number nor did she remember his name and features went unnoticed. She wondered if she would recognize him if she met him again for she had not even bothered to look at him. Nevertheless, she moved on forgetting the stranger and their meeting at the cafe.

"Today we have gathered here for a workshop on the software application process. After this workshop, I guarantee that even the nontech-savvy person would be able to comfortably work and would not be technically handicapped. So let's begin..."

Kirti, one of the attendants of the workshop, was least interested but as it was a part of the company's policy, she had *no option but to sail through the 5 days workshop. Physically present but mentally she was elsewhere. Her aim was market research so that she could get the deal and she wondered how the workshop on software could help. Anyways she had decided to be a part of the workshop but being least interested she placed herself at the back just like the least interested back bencher students. As she was busy with her phone, a familiar tone hit her senses. She knew she had heard the voice before, but she was unable to locate the origin. She sat upright just to get a glance of the speaker, but unfortunately, the figure made no sense but the voice did. While she was trying to connect the possibilities, from out of the blue a hand came towards her and the familiar voice said, "Madam, can I help you?"*

Destiny had a way and Kirti believed that meeting someone again cannot be just a coincidence when the matter was the same as well. "Technical mates" as they termed their relationship as. After the workshop, Amit Tandon and Kirti Ahuja became Technical Mates. They met at the café regularly mostly after the whole day's work. Initially, it was for technical matters but slowly and steadily their relationship took a turn and they met even for non-technical matters as well.

Kirti soon felt comfortable in Amit's presence and wanted to share everything that happened in the day. Unless and until she spoke to him and he comforted her, her day never ended. Though he was a technical person, Kirti felt by nature he was a counselor and so she had no inhibitions sharing her deepest secrets with him and neither did Amit stop her. On a weekday, the meeting was not an issue, but weekends would be an issue for both, as both had their family life, yet they managed an hour or two but the meeting was a must.

****

While she was reliving the past good times with her technical mate, Amit, she had lost touch with time. As soon as she realized it was beyond 10 minutes, she was about to call Amit, when just like a tornado, a hand swayed her towards the corner of the street, rather a dark alley. Before she could react, she was pinned to the wall. She was hurt because the grip was tight making it difficult for her to breathe.

"Amit, that hurts. Leave me. Please. It hurts..."

VI
Scene 6

"Shut up *you bitch. Good for nothing. For everything you need help. Can't stand on your own. What do you think I am? Your servant, at your disposal. You think, I am sitting here idle, who you call anytime whenever you need me. Enough is enough. It is just for these reasons your husband hates you. He does not value you. Mercy him, he does not even know he has a wife who breaks his trust with another man, who she just met and befriended on the streets. What a characterless woman you are. You deserve whatever is happening to you. It is because of this nature of yours, everything you get you loose.*

Madam, I am not the use and throw, just like other relationships of yours. Learn to value someone, if you want others to value you. Don't try to sugarcoat me. Who does not have an issue? Even I have my set of problems, but I don't cry over them with outsiders nor do I find the means to run away from my loved ones. Since you run away, you are a loner. Look outside Madam, everyone has company, but you are all alone here meeting a stranger and making your life miserable. I pity you today. Despite having everything, you still have nothing. A loser is what you are. You deserve to be at the mercy of people.

Everyone should just pity you. As you had rightly said, "You are a burden to any relationship that you come across." God save them.

Don't try to contact me henceforth. If you do, I promise I won't keep quiet. Just like you have the photographs, I have them with me as well and I promise I will destroy you. First of all, you are a loner, just imagine what will happen if I disclose our little secret to your hubby and parents. Goodbye Madam Kirti Ahuja, the loser mate"

****

With a sudden jerk, Amit left Kirti standing in the dark alley. Like a shadow, he was leaving with shades of grey left all over Kirti. She stood there shocked. Her soul was screaming, "Amit... Amit..." but her lips did not move nor there was a sound. Walking with her head bowed down in shame, she wondered what she had done to get to this fate. "Was it her dependency on this new mate" or "her infidelity" that made her stand naked in the middle of the street with nowhere to go?

VII
Scene 7

Kirti was in a daze. She hardly could believe what had happened. She kept saying to herself, *"I was dreaming. Amit will come any moment and we will share a cup of coffee and talk it out like other times."* To her dismay, by the time she neared the café, the owner was pulling down the shutter. The rolling sound brought her to reality. What had happened a few minutes back was a fact. Amit had accused her and left her humiliated in the middle of nowhere. She was unable to fathom what had happened and stood frozen unable to take the next move, but she had to move somewhere. The closed café and dark streets indicated that she had to go back home. In that state of dizziness, she could hear someone calling out to her. *"Bibiji... Idhar aiye.. Bibiji..."* Though she kept walking, a heavily built man stood in front of her from just nowhere.

"Bibiji... Kaha ja rahe hon. Aaj phir Babuji se ladai ho gayi kya. Chaliye, aise ruth kar ghar chod kar nahi jaate. Chaliye" (Did you have a fight with your father again. No problem. Such fights happen between father and daughter. Does that mean you should leave your home and go away? I won't let you go. Let's go home)

For a second it took Kirti to realize that it was Shyamlal Ji, the building security. Already disturbed, Kirti decided to follow Shyamlal ji where ever he was taking her. Caring and full of concern, he helped Kirti to get into the lift, and while she was standing in front of her house, he did not ring the bell for it was too late, but he managed to dodge out the keys from the flower pot and unlocked the door helping Kirti rest herself on the nearby sofa.

As soon as Shyamlal Ji had left closing the main door behind him, Kirti could hear voices from inside the house. She wondered why her Parents were awake at that time of the night. *"Daddy, you have blood pressure and you are suffering from a kidney ailment. The Dr has advised rest, but you are awake for so long. Why? You better sleep now or else you will land up in the hospital tomorrow."* Kirti advised her Daddy half asleep. She was in a state of dizziness and could not move to help her father to the bedroom. Just as she was about to sleep,

"Kirti, what is wrong with you? Again you have fought with jamai babu. Have you called him? Does he know you are here? If not, you better move out right away. Fighting just like a child. I don't know when you will grow up. Beta, I will not let you stay here, especially when you fight and walk out of the house. Get up. Uff, you cannot even stand. Are you drunk?" Saying which Daddy was checking on Kirti, when...

"Daddy, enough. I am not your school-going girl any longer. I am mature enough to make my own decisions and I don't need to prove myself to anyone. Whether I fight with my husband or leave his house and stay where ever it is my decision. Please stop treating me like a school-going girl. Everywhere you don't need to interfere. For now, just leave me alone."

Saying which Kirti took the cushion and burrowed her head under it and ignored her father's constant blabbering.

VIII
Scene 8

After a few hours, she woke up hearing mumbled sounds. It sounded as if somebody was whispering. But who? She could not see any person in flesh and blood but the voices seemed to appear right in front of her. It looked as if there was an opaque wall that only carried the sound. A sudden light out of nowhere made her blink and the next moment, she saw her parents in deep conversation with each other. They were near yet so far and the bright white light blinded her but only her hearing senses were working.

Mummy: *Why are you so rude to her? Why can't you be like other fathers to her? Being friendly yet being strict. Just being strict and always reprimanding her is only pushing you away from her. I know how much you love her, but she feels you are more like Hitler, a rule lover than a father who loves his child.*

Daddy: *Aha!!! Hitler, you said. As a child, I loved that character. The orthodox and authoritarian ruler who everyone was scared of, but ultimately he was able to make his people get results the way he wanted. His way was different and not accepted but results were guaranteed. Sometimes as a Parent, we need to walk on a path that is not accepted and it is for our* *child's better future. I am doing the same and for that even if I am hated I have no regrets. Tomorrow, when we are not there, I don't want Kirti to stumble and feel lonely. She needs to learn to face her battles by herself. One wrong decision and life may take a U-Turn from which one cannot return.*

As a child, I took everything for granted. I was totally dependent on my father. He was a teacher in a government school and unfortunately the only earning member raising a family of 6 members. Then one day all of a sudden he was infected by jaundice and he never recovered. From living in our own 1 BHK, we moved to just one room kitchen, and that too on a rental basis. Mummy was unable to manage the house with a mere housemaid job and that is when the responsibility was thrown on my shoulder. I left my studies and started working as a clerk, educating my siblings thinking that once they settle they will care for me, but as soon as they settled in high-income jobs, they left me and my family to fend for ourselves and do you remember Kirti at that time was just 2 years old. It was a struggle to make ends meet. Yet you did not give up nor did we ask for alms. You took up stitching jobs apart from the nanny's job you were doing which gave me time to finish my graduation and then I took the job of a teacher and somewhat our status improved.

Just as things were settling down, Shankar, my younger brother faced a huge loss because of some investment. He approached me for help. Now being the goody older brother, I helped him financially to be falsely labeled for the money laundering issue, and in the bargain, I lost my job and reputation which affected you and Kirti as well and you both had to leave overnight. While I was serving the punishment behind bars, you struggled to bring up Kirti but did not let anyone know where I was. Somehow you saved Kirti from the fate that society would inflict on her.

It was a struggle, a big one, and all because of my nature of being too humble or good and taking relationships and life for granted. Yet, I did not want Kirti to suffer and hence I was always stringent with her. It labeled me as Hitler but thankfully Kirti is not a replica of my weakness. She knows or at least tries to differentiate between good and bad. The only issue is that she needs to be pushed all the time. The laid-back attitude. Only a kick or a harsh word gets her motivated to prove herself, but those people become a villain in her life. Just like me and our Jamai babu. Anyways, I am sure, one day she will realize all this after we are long gone away."

Tears flowed down her eyes leaving a mark on her cheeks. She wanted to hug her father and tell him how much she loved him. She was so close yet so far. She was unable to reach him. The bright white light was fading and so were her Parents. She tried to hold on to them. She called on to them but they walked away hand in hand and she could do nothing but watch them disappear. The room seemed to be just like the way it was before she saw her Parents. Silent walls were all around her and she was lying down on the sofa with a cushion over her head. Waking up, she went from one room to another but nowhere could she find her Daddy. Even things seemed unfamiliar to her. Suddenly the room seemed unfamiliar to her, yet there was some familiarity. She had been in this house before, but she was unable to recollect when and where. As she delved further her head started to spin and everything around her started to blur. She wanted to be out of the unfamiliar but familiar place. Finding her bag and mobile, she was about to get up from the sofa when TUCK...

she heard the sound of the door unlocking. She knew no one was at home as she had just checked when her Parents suddenly disappeared. So, who was inside the house?

Tuck...

IX

Scene 9

"Happy Anniversary to us. Happy Anniversary to us" he was singing while walking with a bouquet of roses and lilies and with a bottle of wine.

"Hey, Shonna. What happened? What got you so late? Don't tell me you forgot, we had a dinner date today. No worries. Forgotten and forgiven. I have ordered your favourite Chinese food from your favourite Mainland outlet. You look so tired and hence you took a power nap I suppose. Nevertheless, hurry to freshen up or the food will get cold and then you won't enjoy it. We still have some time before the day ends. Hurry, till then let me arrange the table and set forth the glasses as well. It is time to enjoy."

Just as she was heading to the washroom, she glanced back and muttered to herself. "This is so unlikely of Kartik. Something is definitely wrong. Kirti, you better take care of what's at stake for you today."

"Hey, Happy Anniversary. Good wishes for our 10 years of togetherness and many more to come in the future." Saying this Kartik plants a kiss on Kirti's face. While they sip their wine, Kirti is uncomfortable seeing the change in

Kartik's behaviour but she dares not to question him.

Kartik gets up from the table and plays some peppy music. So very, unlikely of him. Whenever Kirti played the dhinchak songs, he would either reprimand her for her taste in music or would simply shut down the system. And here he was playing the system that played loudly Kirti's favourite songs. "I wonder how he knows my favourite songs." While she was lost in her thoughts, Kartik bows down on his knees, "Honey, can I have the honour of dancing with you, my life partner."

While she is grooving step by step with Kartik mesmerised by his change, she stares blankly at him. Her mind raced back and forth. "Let's have dinner dear. The food is cold already. Let's talk while eating as well."

"Kirti dear. You did not tell me how your day was. You had a meeting today to discuss your promotion right? How did it go? Aha!!! You were out at the beach, so probably, it was a good meeting right. What say? Common, hurry, I am dying to know..." Kartik looked encouragingly at his wife. Kirti knew time had come and she would now be the show spoiler. She wished she could hold on to the goody - goody times, but times change and she has to face it. With a trembling heart and weak limbs she moved toward her bag and took out the slip. Just as she was about to show it to Kartik, he was standing right besides her trying to hold her hands and she was shivering. "What is this?"

X
Scene 10

"What is it that you are hiding in that silly folder of yours? Common, show it Kirti. I know it won't be a check of 1 crore. You are not worth even lakhs."

Without waiting a moment for Kirti to turn and hand over what she was holding, Kartik stood behind her and snatched the folder to have a look all by himself.

"Aha!!! I knew. I knew what my wife is capable of. What more could I expect from a loser like you? Someone takes away your project and you stand there dumb as if your mouth has been taped. Everything, especially the donkey work is done by you but your team lead takes the credit and one fault even if it is his, he easily slips the blame on you and you have no words to prove your innocence. So what else could I have expected from you? A promotion letter instead of this pink slip. Here I get awards and recognition and am moving up the ladder and my dear wife is climbing down the ladder in a hurry and I am sure by the time, I am at the top, you would have slipped further down, maybe at the ground level. Probably there would be no company left that would hire you or should I say rejected you or shown you the pink slip? You are shameless, but more than

you it is a matter of shame for me. I mean how, do I introduce you to my circle? Look, there goes my wife who only gets sacked by the company that she toils hard in. Mind you, she is good for nothing. Strives hard but the end result is nothing but a failure.
"

"Enough!!! Kartik. What do you expect? I should work in an organization that does not value me. Someone who steals my work and passes it as theirs or blames me for everything that goes wrong. Stop being so rude. I am already depressed about losing this job and I don't have another one. Again I have to go through the entire process which is so tiring and I don't know where to start even. I don't know where to apply and how..."

"Ha... Ha... Ha... More than you it is tiring for an employer. Imagine the efforts both physically and monetarily and within months the efforts are down the drain. My advice to you will be to stop wasting your time and the employer's time, best will be to sit at home and do some household menial jobs. Oh!!! I forgot you are not good at household jobs as well. The maids do a better job, I think, don't mind."

"Stop it Kartik. One day, I will prove myself and then you would understand my worth." cried Kirti.

"All the best," says Kartik banging the door shut and leaving a teary-eyed Kirti behind.

****

With a trembling heart and wobbly limbs Kirti moves towards her bag and takes out a slip. "Hey what is that?" screams Kartik right from behind Kirti startling her.

"Oh, a pink slip. Nothing to worry. Someone who does not understand your worth and effort is not worthy of you. I still remember how you slogged for 2 days without food and sleep and yet your team lead rejected your work. Such a dumb guy he is. Good that now you are out of that tedious working environment. I don't like to see you struggle so much and what is the use, nothing. Best is that you apply to a company that values their employees and not just use them just like they want. I want you to apply to an organization that is worth your skills. Please don't sit at home and waste your skills. Let me do one thing (keeping his wine glass and removing his laptop). I shall help you search a job that is worth your skills. Kirti come here darling. I am with you. Don't worry. You will get a job worth your skills and I shall....

****

Before Kartik could complete his statement, Kirti picks up her bag and mobile and runs away from the house. She was unable to digest too much of the sugar coated behaviour of her husband.

XI
Scene 11

"Wow, what a pose? Have you got a new job of modelling or acting? I am sure, you would be a failure in that profession also. By the way, must say, good pose with the phone in one hand as if answering a call and one leg hanging in mid-air as if on a footboard, boarding the train. By the way, do you know what is the time? The last local has left long back and now it is time for the first local to start. So are you going to wait for the first local or wishing to board my car so that we can drive back home and rest for sometime till the day begins."

Kartik did not even wait for an answer from his wife Kirti Ahuja. He knew Kirti would follow him to the car.

Silently she walked behind him and tied the seat belt around herself tugging herself to safety and kept looking at Kartik as if trying to ask him a question but hesitated.

"To answer your question how did I find you?

Since you were not home by the time I reached I knew you were out somewhere. First thing I did was checked at Daddy's place, where you generally go visiting your parents when you are upset, but I found the key inside the flower pot so I knew you had not visited the house. The next option was calling your organization whereby they told me that you had left post lunch. You are allergic to the suns heat and so I knew that you would not be roaming the street in the hot sun and so the only place you would hang out is the café, where you did spend time till it was evening. Then you spent time at the beach washing away your pain and then you suddenly realise that it is too late and head towards the station. I tried reaching your phone, but you did not answer, but luckily your GPRS was active and it showed your location. Thanks for giving me a complete night time tour of the city. I must say that now you should apply for a job as a tourist, as you have the pink slip. Something better than the other. Rest is your choice."

Conclusion

Kirti Ahuja, smiled for she knew that she now knew the reality and the meaning of her life. All her questions were answered in a day's journey. All thanks to the pink slip and the last local that took her to various reality journeys uncovering the truth about each phase of life that she faced but could not question.

Though sounds fictional, but an alternate reality or a parallel universe runs along with us, which is nothing but a mirror to what we think and feel. Sometimes living in an alternate reality is a stress buster, which we do through dreams. Yet, we don't remember what we relived during our journey in our alternate reality.

So like, Kirti Ahuja, what is an alternate reality you wish to discover in your life journey?

Please note, being in an alternate reality is not like having an alternate personality or any form of mental illness. Sometimes, you relieve your dreams of being in an alternate reality and it helps you come back with a bang keeping you sane even in times of difficulty.

Hope you like being in the Parallel Universe of Kirti Ahuja. Drop in a review encouraging me on my writing journey. My alternate reality journey as a professional writer.

Know Me

The most difficult part of writing is witing about yourself. Honestly speaking, I don't think I would be able to write my autobiography.

Born in a middle-class Bengali family, I have been brought up in a culturally rich family and values that strives to bring out the best in us as a human. My Parents always stressed being human before any other role we play.

On the professional front, I am a Clinical Psychologist. My career spans a decade working in hospitals and clinics and then in schools as a school counselor. As a child, I was surrounded by books, which helped me develop my reading, communication, and imaginary skills.

As a Mother, I wanted to imbibe the same qualities in my son, especially in reading. In this venture, I started framing new stories that he enjoyed and from there on began my journey into the field of writing, as an author.

I enjoy reading and writing mysteries, especially murder mysteries, as I love reading and following the likes of Agatha Christie, Sherlock Holmes, and Sydney Sheldon. Being a counselor, I have also ventured into self-help books which have been a hit amongst my friends and clients as well.

As an author, I wish to explore other genres as well. Hence, written on the subject of an Alternate Reality.

Meghna As An Author

My writing journey started with a Murder Mystery called **<u>The Murder Weapon.</u>**

The book is about the untimely death of a few businessmen which is termed as suicide but the mysterious way of their death leads a detective to dwell further into the case on his own until he is able to find the murder weapon. The USP of the book is the riddles. Read and decipher the riddles while you read and find out the murder weapon. The book can be found at notionpress.com and also at Amazon.in

Some of my other books include:

- The Deluded Mind
- OSM
- Do you know thy neighbour
- SCAR
- Is the child in you alive
- Happiness in a Jar
- Junior series

Follow me on Facebook: https://www.facebook.com/meauthor1983

Thank you,

Meghna Mukherjee